# FRED Gets Frustrated

Jennifer C. Kelly

Illustrated by Stephen Stone

This is Fred. Fred loves his pet fish Bubbles, silly jokes, and spending time with his best friend, Cali.

## Jennifer C. Kelly - Author

Jennifer is a New Jersey-based member of SCBWI and author of the Fred series. With over two decades as a technology professional, Jennifer has mastered detecting patterns and making the complex simple. She has enjoyed writing since college, first creating poetry and then her debut children's book, Fred Gets Frustrated. Fred is a labor of love and a result of Jennifer's desire to help her son learn emotional intelligence. She is passionate about creating quality content that benefits all families and addresses issues that parents commonly face. Jennifer lives in Wayne with her husband, son, cat, and dog.

IG: @jennifer_c_kelly
ETSY: www.etsy.com/shop/JCKellyStudio
Visit: www.FredTheFrog.net to download the companion calm-down worksheet and coloring kit.

## Stephen Stone - Illustrator

Stephen lives in Derbyshire, England with his wife and slightly aloof orange cat Vincent van Mog. He began his creative career training to be a fashion designer before becoming a university lecturer. Now retired from teaching he works as a professional freelance designer and illustrator. Stephen has published books with many mainstream publishers and indie authors. He has a passion for developing expressive and animated characters that kids will remember for years to come.

www.yellowstonestudio.co.uk

Text copyright © 2021 Jennifer C. Kelly.
Illustrations copyright © 2021 Stephen Stone.
Edited by Brooke Vitale, Jennifer Rees

All rights reserved. No part of this book may be reproduced or transmitted in any form or by any means, electronic or mechanical, including photocopying, recording, or by any information storage and retrieval system, without written permission from the author.
For information address:
JC Kelly Books
PO Box 1421
Wayne, NJ 07474-1421

Published by Jennifer C.Kelly
www.FredTheFrog.net

Library of Congress Cataloging -in Publication-Data
Names: Kelly, Jennifer C - Author / Stone, Stephen - Illustrator
Title: Fred Gets Frustrated, Jennifer C.Kelly, illustrated by Stephen Stone
ISBN 978-1-7376273-3-3(hbk)
ISBN 978-1-7376273-1-9(pbk)

Display type set TOBI Regular
Text type set in Grandstander
Book Design by Stephen Stone

For R.B.K. – Infinity So's.

One sunny morning, Fred was getting ready to bake cookies when he noticed he was out of butter and eggs.

"I'll have to go to the store first," Fred said to Bubbles.

Fred looked and looked but could not find the keys to unlock his scooter.

"Where could they be?" Fred wailed.

# "OH PHOOEY!!!"

Fred shouted, stomping his foot.

Fred was **frustrated**.

Realizing he was getting too upset, Fred paused to think about his favorite joke.

"Why are Pirates called Pirates?

Because they ARRRR!"

"HA, HA, HA!"

Fred laughed.
That joke always made him feel better!

Now, feeling calmer, Fred had another idea: "I'll find my keys later and ride my bike to the store instead." Fred got on his bike and started to ride.

THUMP
THUMP
THUMP

Fred saw that his bike had a flat tire.
"**WHAT?!**" croaked Fred.

"UGGGHHHHHHH!!!"

Fred was **frustrated.** Again.

Noticing he was feeling very upset and wanting to feel better, Fred made his hands into tight fists, squeezing them, to get out some of the frustration.

Finally, he started to feel less angry.
"**It's a nice sunny day,**" Fred said.
"**I can walk to the store.**"

As he walked through the woods, Fred noticed all the things that made him feel happy. He saw flowers, a blue butterfly, some chirping birds, and a pond full of fish with ducks swimming by.

Fred was grateful because these things made him feel better and that made the walk worth it.

At the store, Fred quickly found the butter. He had everything except eggs when he heard someone call, "Hey Fred, it's great to see you!"

It was his friend Cali. "Hi, Cali, I was just getting eggs so I could make cookies for my grandma."

Cali grinned and said, "I'll come with you!"

Fred and Cali walked over to where the eggs should be, but there were no eggs left.

Fred yelled **"WHYYYYY?!"** and began to hop around in anger.

Fred was **really frustrated.**

Cali saw how upset this made Fred and said, "Look, it's OK to be frustrated, but I have an idea that might help.

Take one deep breath in while slowly counting to three. Then count to three again while breathing out. Why don't we try it together right now?"

Fred nodded and they both took a deep breath in while counting to three. Then, slowly, they exhaled.

Fred and Cali felt better.
"Thank you for helping me calm down, Cali," Fred said.

"Now that I feel better, I've come up with a new plan. Let's see if we can find eggs at the market next door!" Fred and Cali bought their groceries and then went to the other store.
"Yay! We found them!" Cali said.

Fred replied, "My grandma will be so happy when I bring her cookies for her birthday tomorrow! Would you like to help me make them?"

"You bet! Let's go bake some cookies!" replied Cali.

Cali and Fred had lots of fun baking.

When the cookies were done, Cali said, "These cookies came out great! It's been a fun day, but I've got to head home now. See you tomorrow!"

As he waved goodbye to Cali, Fred thought
"**Mmmm**, these cookies smell so good.

I'm sure Grandma won't miss just one!"

Excited to eat a warm cookie with a tall glass of milk, he opened the refrigerator. But as he reached inside, his hand knocked over a container, and milk poured out all over Fred.

Fred let out one **big, loud,**
"**ARRRRGGGGG!!!**"

Fred was **frustrated.**

Fred looked around.

In the corner, he saw his calm-down box — a special box he'd filled with things he could read, play with, or look at to help him feel relaxed when he got angry. Fred took a cookie and went over to the box.

He tried to get some of the milk off his arm and onto his cookie, then used a tissue to wipe up the rest. When he sat down, he spied something shiny in the box.

**"Ah-ha! I found the keys to my scooter lock!"**

Fred took a bite of cookie and picked up his favorite joke book from the box. Reading the jokes made Fred laugh.

After some time reading, Fred thought back on his day. He remembered his walk, shopping with Cali, the fun they had baking, and how yummy the cookie was.

"Today was a **GREAT** day!"
Fred said to Bubbles. Bubbles swam in fast circles.

Then Fred remembered how excited he was to surprise his grandma with the cookies for her birthday.
"**Tomorrow will be a great day, too!**"
Fred said with a smile.

# What tools do *you* use to calm down?

## Here are some of my favorite ideas:

A calm-down box.

1...2..3

Counting to three while breathing.

"HA, HA, HA!"

A funny joke!

A good book.

Relaxing my body.

Pausing to remember things that make me happy.

Squeezing my fists.

Listening to music.

# CREATE YOUR OWN

Use these pointers to create your own **calm-down box** with a cardboard box or other container you already have at home.

*Put in things that will make you happy.*

- Your favorite book
- Arts and crafts
- Other favorite activities

Some things I have in my calm-down box are tissues, books, paper, crayons, magnetic sand, and a squeeze ball.

## DECORATE

Decorate the box any way you like. It's up to you! Ask a parent, teacher, or friend for help with finding a box and ideas on what to put inside it.

## VISIT

Remember to visit your **calm-down box** whenever you are feeling frustrated or just need some quiet time.

If you can, create your own list of ways for calming down. Leave it in the box for safekeeping.

*Put your finished calm-down box in a quiet space.*

*I'm so happy to share my favorite calming tools with you!*

Made in the USA
Middletown, DE
02 September 2023

37767413R00018